An Island in the Sun

written by Stella Blackstone
illustrated by Nicoletta Ceccoli

Barefoot Books
Celebrating Art and Story

I spy with my little eye a bird flying by.

I spy with my little eye the sun in the sky and a bird flying by.

I spy with my little eye a dolphin jumping free and the sun in the sky and a bird flying by.

I spy with my little eye an island far from me and a dolphin jumping free and the sun in the sky and a bird flying by.

I spy with my little eye a big tangly tree on an island far from me

and a dolphin jumping free and the sun in the sky and a bird flying by.

I spy with my little eye a beach beside the sea and a big tangly tree on an island far from me and a dolphin jumping free and the sun in the sky and a bird flying by.

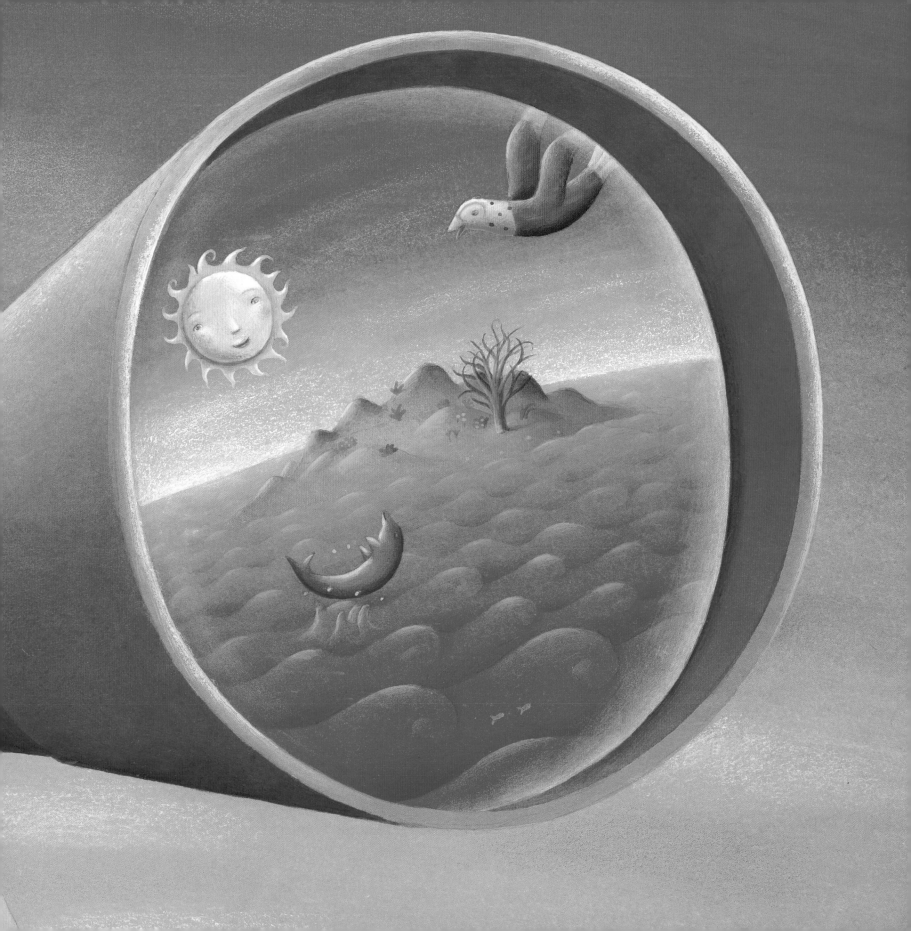

I spy with my little eye someone waiting for me on a beach beside the sea

and a big tangly tree on an island close to me and a dolphin jumping free

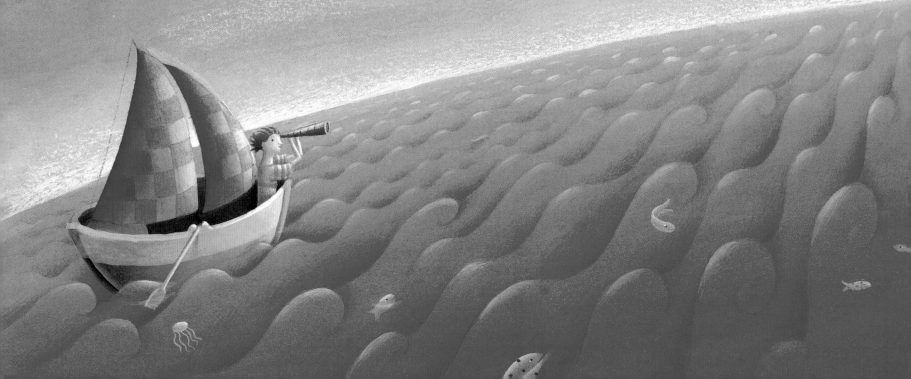

and the sun in the sky and a bird flying by.

Together we laugh, together we play, together we fish 'til the end of the day.

What did I spy with my little eye?

And shall we sail home now, just you and I?

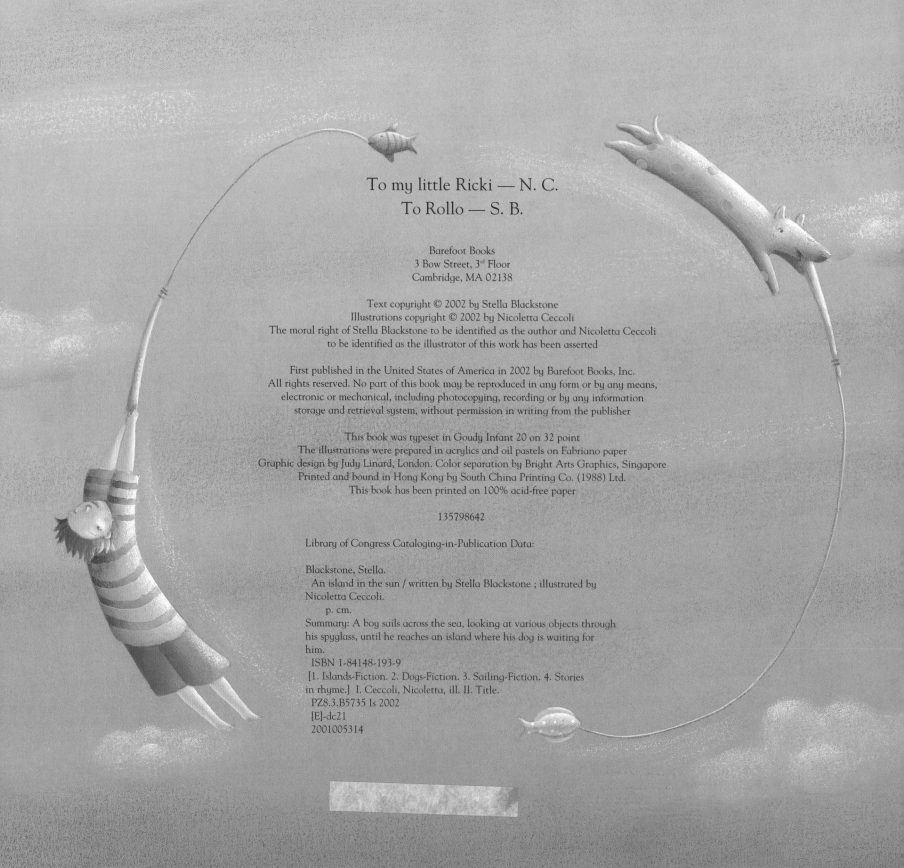

To my little Ricki — N. C.
To Rollo — S. B.

Barefoot Books
3 Bow Street, 3rd Floor
Cambridge, MA 02138

This book was typeset in Goudy Infant 20 on 32 point
The illustrations were prepared in acrylics and oil pastels on Fabriano paper
Graphic design by Judy Linard, London. Color separation by Bright Arts Graphics, Singapore
Printed and bound in Hong Kong by South China Printing Co. (1988) Ltd.
This book has been printed on 100% acid-free paper

135798642

Library of Congress Cataloging-in-Publication Data:

Blackstone, Stella.
  An island in the sun / written by Stella Blackstone ; illustrated by
Nicoletta Ceccoli.
     p. cm.
Summary: A boy sails across the sea, looking at various objects through
his spyglass, until he reaches an island where his dog is waiting for
him.
  ISBN 1-84148-193-9
  [1. Islands-Fiction. 2. Dogs-Fiction. 3. Sailing-Fiction. 4. Stories
in rhyme.] I. Ceccoli, Nicoletta, ill. II. Title.
PZ8.3.B5735 Is 2002
[E]-dc21
2001005314

Barefoot Books
Celebrating Art and Story

At Barefoot Books, we celebrate art and story with books
that open the hearts and minds of children from all walks of life,
inspiring them to read deeper, search further, and explore their own creative gifts.
Taking our inspiration from many different cultures, we focus on themes that encourage
independence of spirit, enthusiasm for learning, and acceptance of other traditions.
Thoughtfully prepared by writers, artists and storytellers from all over the world,
our products combine the best of the present with the best of the past
to educate our children as the caretakers of tomorrow.

www.barefootbooks.com